To CoCo

lots of love

Josie

JOSIE FIRMIN

ORCHARD BOOKS

This book is dedicated to

Olivia, Ruth, Georgia,
Lewis, Sam, Dorian,
Laurence, Alastair
and Steve.

ORCHARD BOOKS
96 Leonard Street, London EC2A 4RH
Orchard Books Australia
14 Mars Road, Lane Cove, NSW 2066
1 85213 699 5
First published in Great Britain 1994
© Josie Firmin

The right of Josie Firmin to be identified as Author of this Work has been
asserted by her in
accordance with the Copyright, Designs and Patents Act, 1988.
A CIP catalogue record for this book is available from the British Library

Printed in Hong Kong

Applauding acrobats

Bouncing babies

Cooking casseroles

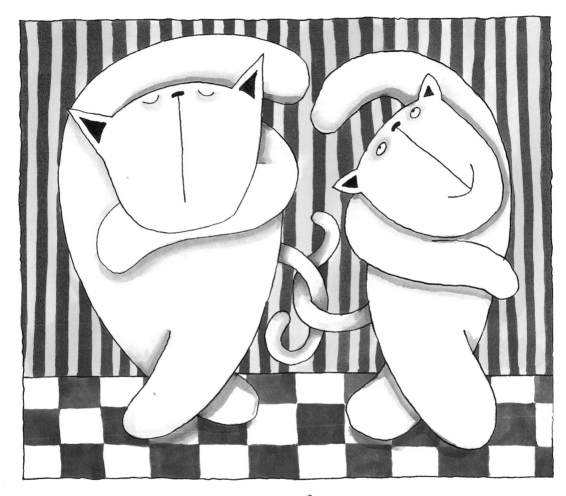

Doing dances

Eating eggs

Finding frogs

Gobbling grapes

Holding hamburgers

Imitating insects

Juggling jesters

Kicking kettles

Licking lollipops

Making messes

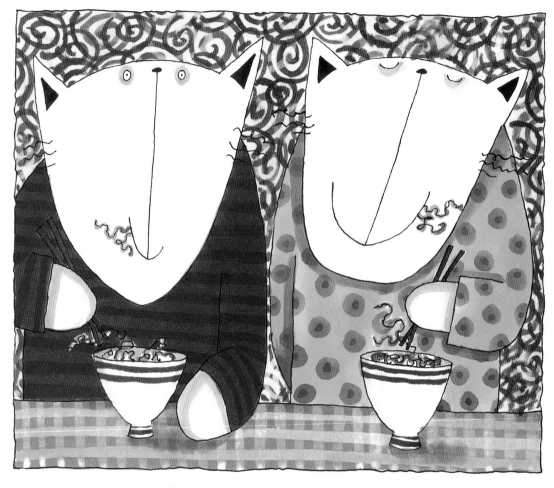

Nibbling noodles

Ordering octopus

Plucking peacocks

Quarrelling queens

Running races

Singing songs

Telling tales

Using umbrellas

Verifying vertebrae

Wearing wigs

X-raying Xerxes

Yawning youths

Zipping zips

Goodnight. Sleep Tight.

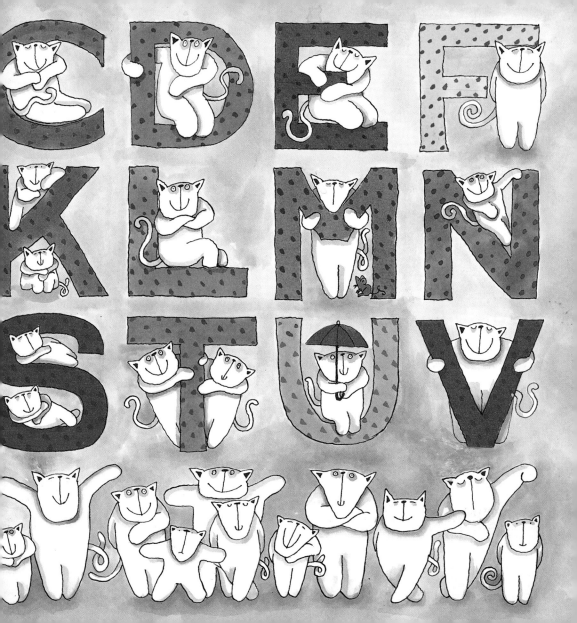